D1179116

A catalogue record for this book is available from the British Library

Published by Ladybird Books Ltd
80 Strand London WC2R ORL
A Penguin Company

2 4 6 8 10 9 7 5 3 1

LADYBIRD and the device of a Ladybird are
trademarks of Ladybird Books Ltd

© Disney MMI

DISNEY'S

ATLANTIS
THE LOST EMPIRE

Ladybird

Milo Thatch worked in the boiler room of a museum. Milo was good at making maps and studying languages from long-lost civilisations. But above all, Milo's dream was to find the lost city of Atlantis.

Milo was in search of *The Shepherd's Journal* – a book that showed the way to the city. Milo knew he could find Atlantis if he could just find the book, but no one believed him. Then one day...

As Milo returned home that evening, someone was waiting for him.

"My name is Helga," the stranger explained. "I have been sent by my employer, who has an interesting mission for you."

Milo followed Helga to Preston Whitmore's mansion. Whitmore was an old friend of Milo's grandfather and he gave Milo his grandfather's most prized possession – *The Shepherd's Journal*! Whitmore wanted Milo to join an expedition to find Atlantis.

A few days later, Milo and Helga boarded a submarine called the *Ulysses*. Whitmore introduced Milo to Commander Rourke, who was in charge.

As the *Ulysses* left the harbour, Milo excitedly told the crew about Atlantis. But the crew wasn't interested in Atlantis, not even when Milo told them about the

Leviathan – a sea
monster that guarded
the entrance to Atlantis!
No one seemed to be
listening until...

The crew heard a strange noise, which grew louder and louder. Suddenly a huge sea monster attacked the submarine – it was the Leviathan!

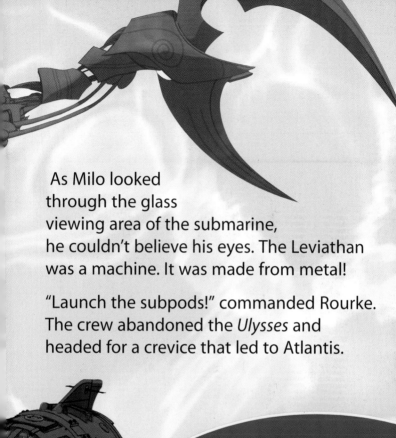

As Milo looked
through the glass
viewing area of the submarine,
he couldn't believe his eyes. The Leviathan
was a machine. It was made from metal!

"Launch the subpods!" commanded Rourke.
The crew abandoned the *Ulysses* and
headed for a crevice that led to Atlantis.

After many days travelling, the crew decided to rest and set up camp in a cave. Milo read *The Shepherd's Journal* over and over. He had to find Atlantis! Just then, one of the tents burst into flames – some fireflies had set the camp alight! "Fire!" Milo shouted.

As the crew ran for cover, one of their vehicles exploded. The ground gave way and everyone slipped into a sleeping volcano!

Milo had fallen into a different part of the volcano and injured himself. When he awoke, he found himself staring at masked warriors! One of them walked towards him and touched the wound on his shoulder. The wound healed instantly!

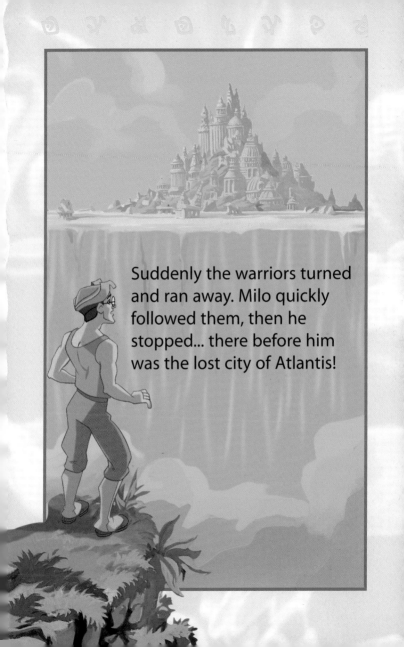

Suddenly the warriors turned and ran away. Milo quickly followed them, then he stopped... there before him was the lost city of Atlantis!

The rest of the crew
caught up with Milo, and
stared at Atlantis and the warriors.
The one who had healed Milo's
wound walked towards them.

It was Princess Kida. "Welcome to Atlantis,"
she said.

Kida took the strangers into Atlantis.
The King was very angry – he didn't trust
strangers. "May we stay just one night, sir?"
asked Rourke.
"Very well," the King replied.

Kida liked the strangers. She thought that they could help unravel the secrets of her people's past. That night she took Milo on a tour of Atlantis and showed him a secret underwater dome.

Milo translated the pictures and words on the dome walls, and told Kida the story of Atlantis.

The story told how the crystals that the Atlanteans wore around their necks were linked to the Mother Crystal – the Heart of Atlantis. Milo realised that the Crystal was keeping the Atlanteans and the city alive!

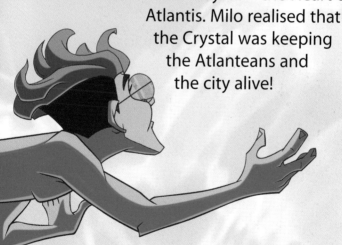

When Milo and Kida left the dome, Rourke was waiting for them. He told Milo that he wanted to steal the Heart of Atlantis.

"That Crystal is the only thing that is keeping these people alive. If you take it away they'll die!" Milo shouted.

But Rourke didn't care. He went to ask the King where to find the Crystal.

The King wouldn't tell him. "You will destroy yourselves!" was all he said.

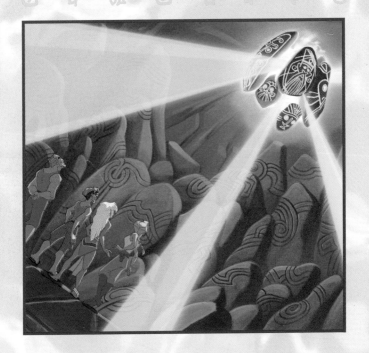

Rourke ignored the King and made his way down into the centre of the city. As Rourke approached the Crystal, it recognised danger and turned red.

The Crystal then sent out a blue light (as it had done all those years before). Looking for royal blood, the light found Kida. She rose into the air and joined with the Crystal.

Rourke took the Heart of Atlantis and the Princess (who were now one) and prepared to leave Atlantis. Milo *had* to do something to save the city. But what? He showed the Atlanteans how to turn on their flying machines – flying fish – and together they went after Rourke.

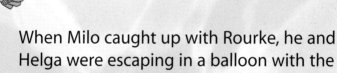

When Milo caught up with Rourke, he and Helga were escaping in a balloon with the pod that held Kida. Milo climbed into the balloon and tried to rescue the pod.

But Milo couldn't reach the pod and Rourke leapt at him. Rourke was about to push him over the edge when Milo scratched Rourke with a piece of the Crystal. Rourke instantly crystallised and fell to the ground, where he broke into tiny pieces. The balloon crashed to the floor, and awoke the volcano…

Milo and his friends returned the crystallised Princess Kida to Atlantis. The Crystal protected the city from the erupting lava. Once the danger was over, the Crystal released the Princess. Atlantis was safe once more.

Milo decided to stay in Atlantis with Kida. The rest of the crew returned home, but they all agreed to keep Atlantis a secret forever – even Mr Whitmore!

Atlantean alphabet

a	b	c	d	e

f	g	h	i	j	k

l	m	n	o	p	q

r	s	t	u	v

w	x	y	z

CH	SH	TH